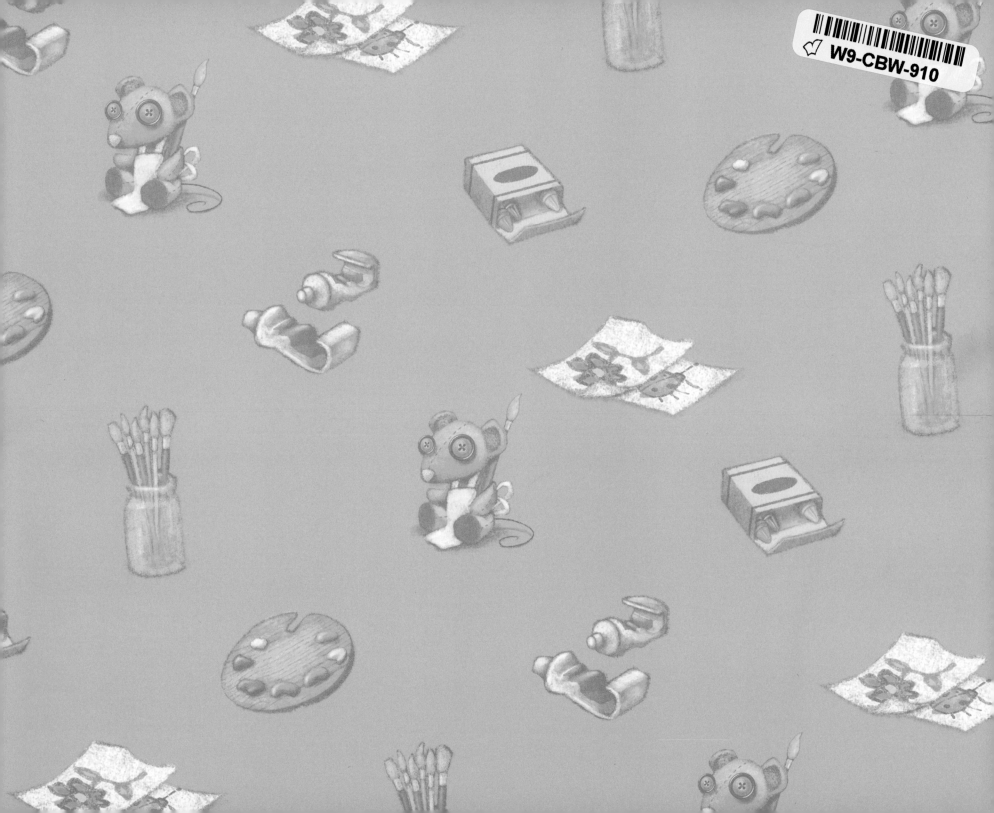

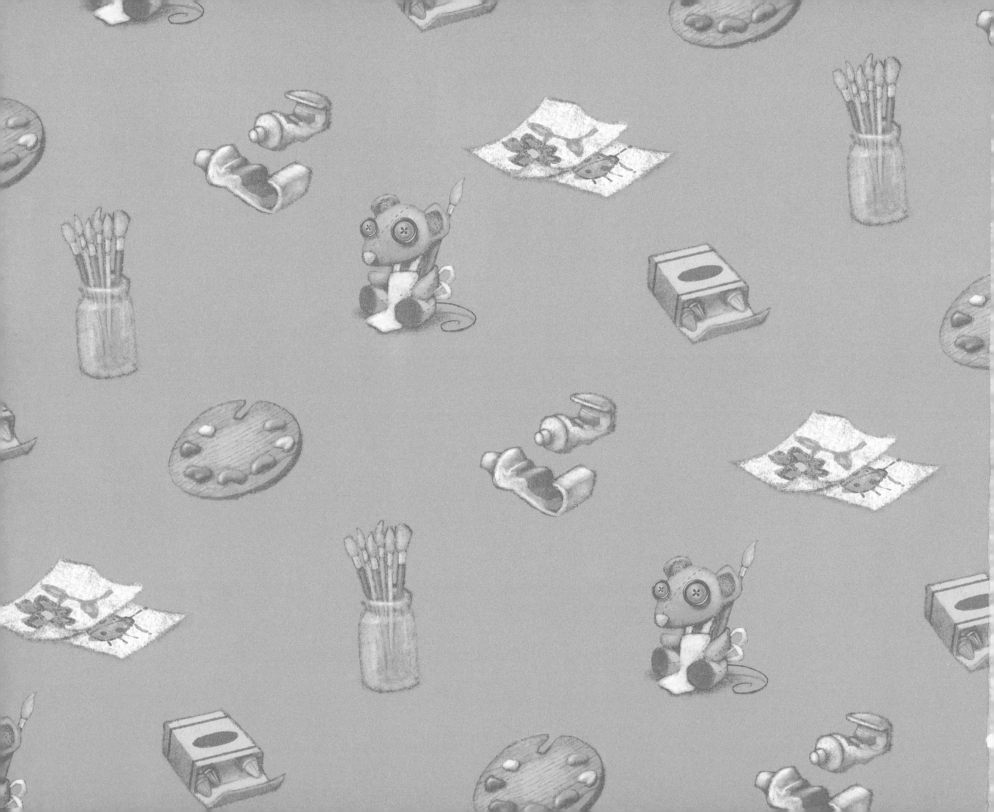

Isabella

Artist Extraordinaire

Just how inspired can a little girl be?

words by Jennifer Fosberry • pictures by Mike Litwin

sourcebooks
jabberwocky

For my family who always believes,
for Mike who makes my ideas beautiful,
and for Dom who let me finish the hat.
—JF

For Glynis, an inspiration to all those around her
and a far more talented artist than I.
—ML

"Isabella, no school today," the father said.
"We should go somewhere special."

"Home is special," said the little girl.

"Yes, but how about the park?"
asked the mother.

"Let me **THINK** about it."

"An *afternoon* in the park would be lovely," said the little girl. "But Alexander's party is there this *Sunday*."

"Good *point*," the mother said.

"What about horseback riding?" the father asked.

"I love horses," said the little girl. "But not today. Let's **CROSS** that idea off the list."

"How about the lake?" the father asked.

"A BOAT PARTY would be fun,"
said the little girl. "But it's awfully chilly today."

"Should we go into the city?" the mother asked.

"We could take the train," the father said.

"A **MODERN**-day adventure," said the little girl. "But home is fun too."

"How about the ballet?"
the mother asked.

"The ballet is beautiful," said the little girl. "But I was under the IMPRESSION I got to pick what we do. Besides, you can just watch my class next week."

"Another good POINTE," the mother said.

"Pick someplace or
we'll be staring at a
STARRY NIGHT
and we won't be going anywhere,"
the father said.

"I know, I know," said the little girl. "There are so many places, I could just

SCREAM."

"We could **HOP** out for some
ice cream," the mother said.

"I love ice cream," said the little girl.
"But maybe we should save that for
another **NIGHT**."

"I suppose we could **POP** down to the store," the mother said.

"A nice warm bowl of **SOUP** sounds great," said the little girl.

"I've got it. I'll do something special for us," said the little girl.

"I'll WHISTLE when I'm ready, MOTHER."

"Voilà! We can go everywhere
and see everything, right here,"
Isabella said.

And the little girl led her family to
a most wondrous place...

A museum of
her own making.

The Thinker
Auguste Rodin
Musée Rodin, Paris, France

A Sunday on La Grande Jatte—1884
Georges Seurat
The Art Institute of Chicago, Chicago, USA

Napoleon Crossing the Alps
Jacques-Louis David
Château de Malmaison, Paris, France

The Boating Party
Mary Cassatt
National Gallery of Art, Washington, DC, USA

Suprematistic Construction
Kazimir Malevich

Dancers in Blue
Edgar Degas
Musée d'Orsay, Paris, France

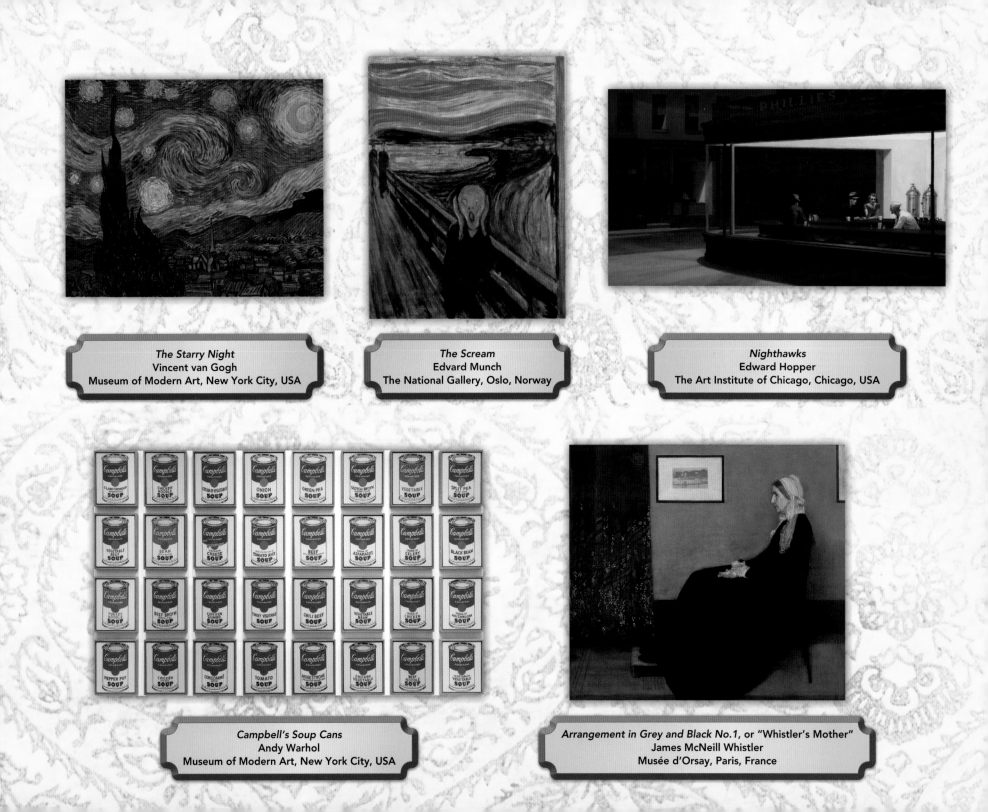

The Starry Night
Vincent van Gogh
Museum of Modern Art, New York City, USA

The Scream
Edvard Munch
The National Gallery, Oslo, Norway

Nighthawks
Edward Hopper
The Art Institute of Chicago, Chicago, USA

Campbell's Soup Cans
Andy Warhol
Museum of Modern Art, New York City, USA

Arrangement in Grey and Black No.1, or "Whistler's Mother"
James McNeill Whistler
Musée d'Orsay, Paris, France

Text © 2019 by Jennifer Fosberry
Illustrations © 2019 by Mike Litwin
Cover and internal design © 2019 by Sourcebooks, Inc.

Sourcebooks and the colophon are registered trademarks of Sourcebooks, Inc.

The art was sketched with blueline pencil and rendered in Adobe Photoshop CC.
The wall art on pages 28-29 was created by Arijá, Lydia, and Alora Litwin.

Page 31 image derived from Andy Warhol Artworks © The Andy Warhol Foundation for the Visual Arts, Inc.

Published by Sourcebooks Jabberwocky, an imprint of Sourcebooks, Inc.
P.O. Box 4410, Naperville, Illinois 60567-4410
(630) 961-3900
Fax: (630) 961-2168
sourcebooks.com

Library of Congress Cataloging-in-Publication Data is on file with the publisher.

Source of Production: Leo Paper, Heshan City, Guangdong Province, China
Date of Production: February 2019
Run Number: 5013139

Printed and bound in China.
LEO 10 9 8 7 6 5 4 3 2 1

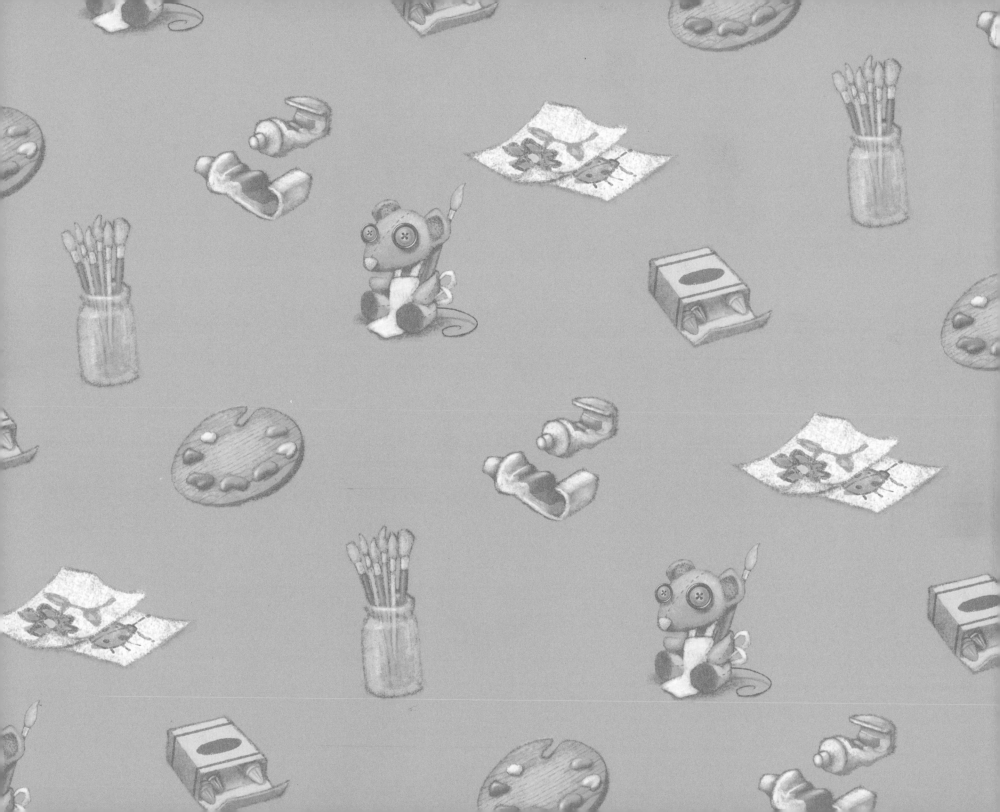